ALSO BY MYRA COHN LIVINGSTON

HIGGLEDY-PIGGLEDY:
VERSES AND PICTURES

MONKEY PUZZLE AND OTHER POEMS

REMEMBERING AND OTHER POEMS

THERE WAS A PLACE AND OTHER POEMS

WORLDS I KNOW AND OTHER POEMS
(Margaret K. McElderry Books)

BIRTHDAY POEMS

CELEBRATIONS

THE CHILD AS POET:
MYTH OR REALITY?

A CIRCLE OF SEASONS

CLIMB INTO THE BELL TOWER:
ESSAYS ON POETRY

EARTH SONGS

MY HEAD IS RED AND OTHER RHYMES

SEA SONGS

SKY SONGS

A SONG I SANG TO YOU

SPACE SONGS

UP IN THE AIR

I LIKE YOU,
IF YOU LIKE ME

I LIKE YOU, IF YOU LIKE ME
Poems of Friendship

Selected and edited by
Myra Cohn Livingston

Margaret K. McElderry Books

NEW YORK

For Margaret K. McElderry

Margaret K. McElderry Books
Macmillan Publishing Company
866 Third Avenue
New York, N.Y. 10022
Collier Macmillan Canada, Inc.

Composition by PennSet, Inc.
Bloomsburg, Pennsylvania
Printed and bound by R. R. Donnelley & Sons
Harrisonburg, Virginia
Designed by Barbara A. Fitzsimmons
Printed in the United States of America
10 9 8 7 6 5 4

Library of Congress Cataloging-in-Publication Data

I like you, if you like me.

Includes index.
Summary: A collection of ninety poems about
friendship by both contemporary and traditional
poets, divided into nine sections reflecting the
diversity of feelings and thoughts on the subject.
1. Friendship—Juvenile poetry. 2. Children's
poetry. [1. Friendship—Poetry. 2. Poetry—
Collections] I. Livingston, Myra Cohn.
PN6110.F8I18   1987   808.81'9353   86-21108
ISBN 0-689-50408-X

ACKNOWLEDGMENTS

The editor and publisher thank the following for permission to reprint the copyrighted material listed below:

ATHENEUM PUBLISHERS, INC. for Patricia Hubbell, "Conjugation" from *The Apple Vendor's Fair*. Copyright © 1963 Patricia Hubbell. X. J. Kennedy, "Agnes Snaggletooth" from *The Forgetful Wishing Well: Poems for Young People*. Copyright © 1985 X. J. Kennedy. (A Margaret K. McElderry Book). Myra Cohn Livingston, "Lonesome" and "We Could Be Friends" from *The Way Things Are and Other Poems*. Copyright © 1974 Myra Cohn Livingston. (A Margaret K. McElderry Book). Eve Merriam, "Secret Talk" from *A Word or Two With You*. Copyright © 1981 Eve Merriam. W. S. Merwin, "Separation" from *The Moving Target*. Copyright © 1963 W. S. Merwin. Lilian Moore, "Letter to a Friend" from *Sam's Place*. Copyright © 1973 Lilian Moore. Zilpha Keatley Snyder, "Today Is Saturday" from *Today Is Saturday*. Copyright © 1969 Zilpha Keatley Snyder.

GWENDOLYN BROOKS for "Pete at the Zoo" from *The Bean Eaters*. Copyright © 1960 by Gwendolyn Brooks.

DELACORTE PRESS/SEYMOUR LAWRENCE for "Coati-Mundi" and "Giraffe" excerpted from the book *Laughing Time* by William Jay Smith. Copyright © 1953, 1955, 1956, 1957, 1959, 1968, 1974, 1977, 1980 by William Jay Smith.

EMANUEL DI PASQUALE for "Letter from Sicily." Copyright © 1987 by Emanuel Di Pasquale.

DODD, MEAD & COMPANY, INC. for "Sensitive Sydney" from *Nautical Lays of a Landsman* by Wallace Irwin and "The Duck and the Kangaroo" and "The Quangle Wangle's Hat" from *The Complete Nonsense Book* by Edward Lear.

DOUBLEDAY & COMPANY, INC. for "Celebration" by Alonzo Lopez and "You Smiled" by Calvin O'John from the book *The Whispering Wind* edited by Terry Allen. Copyright © 1972 by the Institute of American Indian Arts.

DUCKWORTH AND COMPANY, LTD. for "The Fresh Air" by Harold Monro.

PAUL S. ERIKSSON, PUBLISHER for "Misery is" from *Black Misery* by Langston Hughes, copyright 1969.

FARRAR, STRAUS & GIROUX, INC. for "Friendship," "The Song of a Dream," and "I Cannot Forget You" from *In the Trail of the Wind* by John Bierhorst. Copyright © 1971 by John Bierhorst. "Two Friends" from *Spin a Soft Black Song* by Nikki Giovanni. Copyright © 1971 by Nikki Giovanni. "The Owl's Bedtime Story" from *Complete Poems* by Randall Jarrell. Copyright © 1969 by Mrs. Randall Jarrell.

ROBERT FROMAN for "Undefeated" from *Street Poems*. Copyright © 1971 by Robert Froman.

HARCOURT, BRACE, JOVANOVICH, INC. for "Fifty-fifty" from *Honey and Salt* by Carl Sandburg, copyright © 1963 by Carl Sandburg and "They Ask: Is God, Too, Lonely?" from *Good Morning, America* by Carl Sandburg, copyright © 1928, 1956 by Carl Sandburg. "What is the Opposite of Two?" from *Opposites* by Richard Wilbur, copyright © 1973 by Richard Wilbur. "The Marmalade Man Makes a Dance to Mend Us" from *A Visit to William Blake's Inn*, copyright © 1981 by Nancy Willard.

🐚 TABLE OF CONTENTS 🐚

I LIKE YOU,
IF YOU LIKE ME

ONE
"Lonesome All Alone"

What is the opposite of *two*?
A lonely me, a lonely you.

Richard Wilbur

HOPE

Sometimes when I'm lonely,
Don't know why,
Keep thinkin' I won't be lonely
By and by.

Langston Hughes

PETE AT THE ZOO

I wonder if the elephant
Is lonely in his stall
When all the boys and girls are gone
And there's no shout at all,
And there's no one to stamp before,
No one to note his might.
Does he hunch up, as I do,
Against the dark of night?

Gwendolyn Brooks

UNDEFEATED

little   square   of   earth
sidewalk   forgot   to   cover.
                  Lost.
                  Alone.
\\/weeds \\l/ıı   start \\l.l coming ıluı/ up.

Robert Froman

LONELY MONDAY

I would go round and round
     Whispering names,
     Hiding, laughing,
     Making up games,
     Dressing up dolls
Come down from my shelf,
      But I am alone
With the wind and myself.

  Grey pillows of clouds,
    Grey sheets of rain—
       I am the streaks
       On my windowpane.

J. Patrick Lewis

LONESOME

Lonesome all alone
Listens for the phone.

Listens for a call,
Anyone at all.

Listens for a ring,
Saying anything.

Lonesome all alone
Listens for the phone.

Myra Cohn Livingston

LONELINESS

Still, still, stillness
In my head, in my heart.
          Is there anyone there?
          Is there anyone there?
The world's outside
And I want to be a part.
          Is there anyone there?
          Is there anyone there?
There's a coldness inside,
It's so very wintery.
I'm here. *Here* I am,
Alone and lonely.
          Is there anyone there?
          Is there anyone there
          For me?

Felice Holman

THEY ASK: IS GOD, TOO, LONELY?

When God scooped up a handful of dust,
And spit on it, and molded the shape of man,
And blew a breath into it and told it to walk—
That was a great day.

And did God do this because He was lonely?
Did God say to Himself he must have company
And therefore He would make man to walk the earth
And set apart churches for speech and song with God?

These are questions.
They are scrawled in old caves.
They are painted in tall cathedrals.
There are men and women so lonely they believe
    God, too, is lonely.

Carl Sandburg

TWO
"Would You Come and Be My Friend"

THE QUESTION

1

If I could teach you how to fly
Or bake an elderberry pie
Or turn the sidewalk into stars
Or play new songs on an old guitar
Or if I knew the way to heaven,
The names of night, the taste of seven
And owned them all, to keep or lend—
Would you come and be my friend?

2

You cannot teach me how to fly.
I love the berries but not the pie.
The sidewalks are for walking on,
And an old guitar has just one song.
The names of night cannot be known,
The way to heaven cannot be shown.
You cannot keep, you cannot lend—
But still I want you for my friend.

?

Dennis Lee

If the ocean was milk
And the bottom was cream,
I'd dive for you
Like a submarine.

Autograph Verse

THE OWL'S BEDTIME STORY

There was once upon a time a little owl.
He lived with his mother in a hollow tree.
On winter nights he'd hear the foxes howl,
He'd hear his mother call, and he would see
The moonlight glittering upon the snow:
How many times he wished for company
As he sat there alone! He'd stand on tiptoe,
Staring across the forest for his mother,
And hear her far away; he'd look below
And see the rabbits playing with each other
And see the ducks together on the lake
And wish that he'd a sister or a brother:
Sometimes it seemed to him his heart would break.
The hours went by, slow, dreary, wearisome,
And he would watch, and sleep a while, and wake—
"Come home! Come home!" he'd think; and she would
    come
At last, and bring him food, and they would sleep.
Outside the day glared, and the troublesome
Sounds of the light, the shouts and caws that keep
An owl awake, went on; and, dark in daylight,
The owl and owlet nestled there. But one day, deep
In his dark dream, warm, still, he saw a white
Bird flying to him over the white wood.
The great owl's wings were wide, his beak was bright.
He whispered to the owlet: "You have been good
A long time now, and waited all alone
Night after long night. We have understood;

And you shall have a sister of your own,
A friend to play with, if, now, you will fly
From your warm nest into the harsh unknown
World the sun lights." Down from the bright sky
The light fell, when at last the owlet woke.
Far, far away he heard an owlet cry.
The sunlight blazed upon a broken oak
Over the lake, and as he saw the tree
It seemed to the owlet that the sunlight spoke.
He heard it whisper: "Come to me! O come to me!"
The world outside was cold and hard and bare;
But at last the owlet, flapping desperately,
Flung himself out upon the naked air
And lurched and staggered to the nearest limb
Of the next tree. How good it felt to him,
That solid branch! And there in that green pine,
How calm it was, how shadowy and dim!
But once again he flapped into the sunshine—
Through all the tumult of the unfriendly day,
Tree by tree by tree, along the shoreline
Of the white lake, he made his clumsy way.
At the bottom of the oak he saw a dead
Owl in the snow. He flew to where it lay
All cold and still; he looked at it in dread.
Then something gave a miserable cry—
There in the oak's nest, far above his head,
An owlet sat. He thought: The nest's too high,

I'll never reach it. "Come here!" he called. "Come here!"
But the owlet hid. And so he had to try
To fly up—and at last, when he was near
And stopped, all panting, underneath the nest
And she gazed down at him, her face looked dear
As his own sister's, it was the happiest
Hour of his life. In a little, when the two
Had made friends, they started home. He did his best
To help her: lurching and staggering, she flew
From branch to branch, and he flapped at her side.
The sun shone, dogs barked, boys shouted—on they flew.
Sometimes they'd rest; sometimes they would glide
A long way, from a high tree to a low,
So smoothly—and they'd feel so satisfied,
So grown-up! Then, all black against the snow,
Some crows came cawing, ugly things! The wise
Owlets sat still as mice; when one big crow
Sailed by, a branch away, they shut their eyes
And looked like lumps of snow. And when the night,
The friend of owls, had come, they saw the moon rise
And there came flying to them through the moonlight
The mother owl. How strong, how good, how dear
She did look! "Mother!" they called in their delight.
Then the three sat there just as we sit here,
And nestled close, and talked—at last they flew

Home to the nest. All night the mother would appear
And disappear, with good things; and the two
Would eat and eat and eat, and then they'd play.
But when the mother came, the mother knew
How tired they were. "Soon it will be day
And time for every owl to be in his nest,"
She said to them tenderly; and they
Felt they were tired, and went to her to rest.
She opened her wings, they nestled to her breast.

Randall Jarrell

MISS M.F.H.E.I.I. JONES

Melissa Finnan Haddie
Eevy Ivy Ipswich Jones
Used to sit and sigh and cry
On solitary stones.
"No one, no one, no one
Will play with me," she said.
"I wish my name were
Lillian or Lindabelle instead
Of what it is.
For then you see
The others would not laugh at me
And point and snicker when I pass.
Oh, woe is me," said she,
"Alas."

Well, one day when Melissa
Was wandering through town
She chanced upon a baby
Who was just about to drown.
She took her shoes and stockings off
And jumping from the spot,
She dived right in
And soaked her skin
And saved the tiny tot.

Then everybody thanked her
And the children who were mean
Turned suddenly quite purple
And then at once pale green,

And they said to her,
"Melissa, please come and join our games.
You know," they said,
"You really have
A lovely set of names."

Karla Kuskin

DOOR NUMBER FOUR

Above my uncle's grocery store
is a pintu,
is a door.
On the pintu
is a number,
nomer empat,
number four.
In the door
there is a key.
Turn it,
enter quietly.
Hush hush, diam-diam,
quietly.
There, in lamplight,
you will see
a friend,
teman,
a friend
who's me.

Charlotte Pomerantz

WE COULD BE FRIENDS

We could be friends
Like friends are supposed to be.
You, picking up the telephone
Calling me

       to come over and play
       or take a walk,
       finding a place
       to sit and talk,

Or just goof around
Like friends do,
Me, picking up the telephone
Calling you.

Myra Cohn Livingston

Read	see	that	me
up	will	I	like
and	you	like	you
down	and	you	if

Autograph Verse

EVERETT ANDERSON'S FRIEND

Someone new has come to stay
in 13A, in 13A
and Everett Anderson's Mama and he
can't wait to see, can't wait to see
whether it's girls or
whether it's boys and
how are their books and
how are their toys and
where they've been and
where they go and
who are their friends and
the people they know,
oh, someone new has come to stay
next door in 13A.

If not an almost
brother,
why not something
other
like a bird or
a cat or
a cousin or
a dozen uncles?

Please,
says Everett Anderson softly,
why did they have to be
a family of
shes?

Girls named Maria who
win at ball
are not a bit of fun
at all.
No, girls who can run
are just no fun
thinks Everett Anderson!

In 14A when Mama's at work
sometimes Joe and sometimes Kirk
can come till she gets home and be
Everett Anderson's company.

Three boys are just the right amount
for playing games that count,
there isn't any room, you see,
for girls named Maria in company.

If Daddy was here
he would let me in and
call me a careless boy
and then
(even though I
forgot my key)
he would make peanut butter
and jelly for me,
and not be mad
and I'd be glad.

If Daddy was here

he could let me in
thinks Everett Anderson
again.

A girl named Maria
is good to know
when you haven't got
any place to go
and you forgot your
apartment key.

Why, she can say,
"Come in with me,
and play in 13A and wait
if your Mama is working late."

Even if she beats at races it's
nicer to lose in familiar places.

Maria's Mama makes little pies
called *Tacos*,
calls little boys *Muchachos*,
and likes to thank the *Dios*;
oh, 13A is a lovely surprise
to Everett Anderson's eyes!

Everett Anderson's Mama is mad
because he lost the key he had;
but a boy has so many things to do
he can't remember them and keys, too.

And if Daddy were here he would say,
"We'll talk about it another day,"
thinks the boy who got a fussing at
for just a little thing like that.

A girl named Maria
who wins at ball
is fun to play with
after all
and Joe and Kirk and
Maria too
are just the right number
for things to do.

Lose a key,
win a friend,
things have a way of
balancing out,
Everett Anderson's Mama explains,
and that's what the world is all about.

And the friends we find
are full of surprises
Everett Anderson realizes.

Lucille Clifton

THREE
"The Friendly Beasts"

VERN

When walking in a tiny rain
Across the vacant lot,
A pup's a good companion—
If a pup you've got.

And when you've had a scold,
And no one loves you very,
And you cannot be merry,
A pup will let you look at him,
And even let you hold
His little wiggly warmness—

And let you snuggle down beside.
Nor mock the tears you have to hide.

Gwendolyn Brooks

THE TWO CATS

I'm very good friends with both our cats,
I've known them since they were kittens.
And one is little and one has big paws,
And their names are Midget and Mittens.

But sometimes at dusk when we're driving home
And come on the cats by surprise,
I feel a shiver go down my back
Facing their burning eyes.

Elizabeth Coatsworth

FRIEND

When
he wills
his quills
to stand on
end

I'm very glad
that
I'm a friend

of
Porcupine.

Lilian Moore

COATI-MUNDI

As I went walking one fine Sunday,
I happened to meet a Coati-Mundi.
    "Coati-Mundi," I said,
    "It's a lovely Sunday
As sure as you're a Coati-Mundi,
A handsome long-tailed Coati-Mundi
    With eyes peering out,
    A flexible snout,
And a raccoon coat all furry and bundly!"

"I quite agree," said the Coati-Mundi,
"It is indeed a most beautiful Sunday.
    What joy for the eye!
    What clouds! What sky!
    What fields of rye!
    Oh, never have I
In all my life seen such a Sunday!"

So he took my hand, and we walked together,
I and my friend, the Coati-Mundi,
Enjoying that most unusual weather,
Enjoying that most delightful Sunday.

William Jay Smith

BUYING A PUPPY

"Bring an old towel," said Pa,
"And a scrap of meat from the pantry.
We're going out in the car, you and I,
Into the country."

I did as he said, although
I couldn't see why he wanted
A scrap of meat and an old towel.
Into the sun we pointed

Our Ford, over the green hills.
Pa sang. Larks bubbled in the sky.
I took with me all my cards—
It was my seventh birthday.

We turned down a happy lane,
Half sunlight, half shadow,
And saw at the end a white house
In a yellow meadow.

Mrs. Garner lived there. She was tall.
She gave me a glass of milk
And showed me her black spaniel.
"Her name is Silk,"

Mrs. Garner said. "She's got
Three puppies, two black, one golden.
Come and see them." Oh,
To have one, one of my own!

"You can choose one," said Pa.
I looked at him. He wasn't joking.
I could scarcely say thank you,
I was almost choking.

It was the golden one. He slept
On my knee in the old towel
All the way home. He was tiny,
But he didn't whimper or howl,

Not once. That was a year ago,
And now I'm eight.
When I get home from school
He'll be waiting behind the gate,

Listening, listening hard,
Head raised, eyes warm and kind;
He came to me as a gift
And grew into a friend.

Leslie Norris

THE ERIE CANAL

I've got a mule, her name is Sal,
Fifteen years on the Erie Canal.
She's a good old worker and a good old pal,
Fifteen years on the Erie Canal.
We've hauled some barges in our day,
Filled with lumber, coal and hay.
And every inch of the way I know
From Albany to Buffalo.

Low bridge, everybody down!
Low bridge, for we're comin' to a town!
You can always tell your neighbor, can always tell your
   pal,
If you've ever navigated on the Erie Canal.

We'd better look for a job, old gal,
Fifteen years on the Erie Canal.
You bet your life I wouldn't part with Sal,
Fifteen years on the Erie Canal.
Giddap there, Sal, we've passed that lock,
We'll make Rome 'fore six o'clock,
So one more trip and then we'll go
Right straight back to Buffalo.

Low bridge, everybody down!
Low bridge, for we're comin' to a town!
You can always tell your neighbor, can always tell your
   pal,
If you've ever navigated on the Erie Canal.

Where would I be if I lost my pal?
Fifteen years on the Erie Canal.
Oh, I'd like to see a mule as good as Sal,
Fifteen years on the Erie Canal.
A friend of mine once got her sore,
Now he's got a broken jaw,
'Cause she let fly with her iron toe
And kicked him into Buffalo.

Low bridge, everybody down!
Low bridge, for we're comin' to a town!
You can always tell your neighbor, can always tell your
    pal,
If you've ever navigated on the Erie Canal.

Author unknown

THE FRIENDLY BEASTS

Jesus, our brother, kind and good,
Was humbly born in a stable rude;
The friendly beasts around Him stood,
Jesus, our brother, kind and good.

"I," said the donkey, shaggy and brown,
"I carried His mother up hill and down;
I carried her safely to Bethlehem town.
I," said the donkey, shaggy and brown.

"I," said the cow, all white and red,
"I gave Him my manger for His bed;
I gave Him my hay to pillow His head.
I," said the cow, all white and red.

"I," said the sheep with curly horn,
"I gave Him my wool for a blanket warm;
He wore my coat on Christmas morn.
I," said the sheep with curly horn.

"I," said the camel yellow and black,
"Over the desert upon my back,
I brought Him a gift in the wise man's pack.
I," said the camel yellow and black.

"I," said the dove from the rafters high,
"I cooed Him to sleep so He would not cry,
I cooed Him to sleep, my mate and I.
I," said the dove from the rafters high.

And every beast, by some good spell,
In the stable dark was glad to tell,
Of the gift he gave Immanuel,
The gift he gave Immanuel.

English, traditional

THREE

We were just three,
Two loons and me.
They swam and fished,
I watched and wished,
That I, like them, might dive and play
In icy waters all the day.
I watched and wished. I could not reach
Where they were, till I tried their speech,
And something in me helped, so I
Could give their trembling sort of cry.
One loon looked up and answered me.
He understood that we were three.

Elizabeth Coatsworth

FOUR
"One Good Friendship"

Of the islands, Puerto Rico
Of countries, Peru
And of all my friends,
The sweetest is you.

De las islas Puerto Rico
De los paises el Perú
Y de todas mis amigas
La más dulce eres tú.

Autograph Verse

WHAT JOHNNY TOLD ME

I went to play with Billy. He
Threw my cap into a tree.
I threw his glasses in the ditch.
He dipped my shirt in a bucket of pitch.
I hid his shoes in the garbage can.
And then we heard the ice cream man.
So I bought him a cone. He bought me one.
A true good friend is a lot of fun!

John Ciardi

SECRET TALK

I have a friend
and sometimes we meet
and greet each other
without a word.

We walk through a field
and stalk a bird
and chew a blade of
pungent grass.

We let time pass
for a golden hour
while we twirl a flower
of Queen Anne's lace

or find a lion's face
shaped in a cloud
that's drifting, sifting
across the sky.

There's no need to say,
"It's been a fine day"
when we say goodbye:
when we say goodbye
we just wave a hand
and we understand.

Eve Merriam

TWO FRIENDS

lydia and shirley have
two pierced ears and
two bare ones
five pigtails
two pairs of sneakers
two berets
two smiles
one necklace
one bracelet
lots of stripes and
one good friendship

Nikki Giovanni

BETSY JANE'S SIXTH BIRTHDAY

"I should like to buy you a birthday present," said Billy
   to Betsy Jane,
"I should like to buy you a motorcar, a ship and a
   railway train.
I should like to buy you a rose-red ribbon to stick on
   your hair or hat;
But I've only a penny left in my purse, and I can't buy
   much for that."
"But that's all right," said Betsy Jane. "In mine, there's
   a shilling or two.
I think you had better take *my* purse. I should *like* a
   present from you."
So putting their golden heads together it all came right
   as rain;
And the happiest eyes in the world that day were the
   eyes of Betsy Jane.

Alfred Noyes

PUZZLE

My best friend's name is Billy
But his best friend is Fred
and Fred's is Willy Wiffleson
And Willy's best is Ted.
Ted's best pal is Samuel
While Samuel's is Paul. . . .
It's funny Paul says I'm his best—
I hate him most of all.

Arnold Spilka

A BOY'S SONG

Where the pools are bright and deep,
Where the grey trout lies asleep,
Up the river and over the lea,
That's the way for Billy and me.

Where the blackbird sings the latest,
Where the hawthorn blooms the sweetest,
Where the nestlings chirp and flee,
That's the way for Billy and me.

Where the mowers mow the cleanest,
Where the hay lies thick and greenest,
There to track the homeward bee,
That's the way for Billy and me.

Where the hazel bank is steepest,
Where the shadow falls the deepest,
Where the clustering nuts fall free,
That's the way for Billy and me.

Why the boys should drive away
Little sweet maidens from their play,
Or love to banter and fight so well,
That's the thing I never could tell.

But this I know, I love to play
Through the meadow, among the hay;
Up the water and over the lea,
That's the way for Billy and me.

James Hogg

NEIGHBORS

The Cobbles live in the house next door,
In the house with the prickly pine.
Whenever I see them, they ask, "How are you?"
And I always answer, "I'm fine."
And I always ask them, "Is Jonathan home?"
(Jonathan Cobble is nine.)
I'm Jonathan Cobble's very best friend
And Jonathan Cobble is mine.

Mary Ann Hoberman

WITH MY FOOT IN MY MOUTH

The reason I clobbered
Your door like that,
Is cause it's time
We had a chat.

But don't start getting
Talkative—
I've got a speech
I want to give:

"A person needs
A pal alot,
And a pal is what
I'm glad I've got,

So thank you. Thank you."
There, it's said!
I feel my earlobes
Getting red,

And I wish you wouldn't
Grin that way!
It isn't healthy,
Night or day.

But even though
You're such a jerk,
With your corny jokes
And your goofy smirk,

I'm sort of glad
You're my old pard.
You're cheaper than
A bodyguard,

And smaller than a
Saint Bernard,
And cleaner than a
Wrecker's yard.

I like the way
You save on socks:
You wear them till they're
Hard as rocks.

And I think those missing
Teeth are keen:
Your mouth looks like
A slot machine

And every time
I see you grin,
I stick another
Quarter in.

You make me laugh
Till we trip on chairs;
One day we nearly
Fell downstairs.

But I think you're kind of
Brave, I guess:
Your no means no,
Your yes means yes,

And even if
It makes you shrink,
You say the things
You really think.

In fact your mouth
Is never closed—
Your tonsils blush,
They're so exposed.

And your tweety voice
Is never quiet;
They must put birdseed
In your diet.

Still, you seem to know,
When we kid alot,
A time for kidding
A time for not—

Cause often things
I say to you,
I'd ache if any
Body knew.

You choke me up,
You make me sneeze,
I've caught you like
A rare disease:

I'd like to come and
Rub your back;
I'd like to feed you
Crackerjack

And send you messages
In code
And walk along you
Like a road

And bathe you till your
Fleas are gone
And stuff you like
A mastodon,

And let's go play
In Kendal Park;
There's still an hour
Before it's dark.

Cause some things last and
Some things end—
I want you always
For my friend.

Dennis Lee

FIVE
"Come Over"

Well! Hello down there,
friend snail! When did you arrive
in such a hurry?

Issa
translated by Harry Behn

There are gold ships,
There are silver ships,
But there's no ship
Like friendship.

Autograph Verse

HENRY AND MARY

Henry was a young king,
      Mary was his queen;
He gave her a snowdrop
      On a stalk of green.

Then all for his kindness
      and all for his care
She gave him a new-laid egg
      In the garden there.

"Love, can you sing?"
              "I cannot sing."
   "Or tell a tale?"
              "Not one I know."
"Then let us play at queen and king
      As down the garden walks we go."

Robert Graves

A SECRET PLACE

Sit here.
I will build you into a house
of junk from the heap next door.
Don't move.
The pieces are balanced just right
on the porch rail and chair and the floor.
And be as soft as a butterfly
so the neighbors won't come out and look
and you will have a secret place
to read your comic book.

Judith W. Steinbergh

FRIEND

Do you know Paul, Paul Pine (he's nine)
He's really quite . . . unusual.
(The Paul in the house that's next to mine.)
There's something about him that's specially . . . Paul.

> Paul has a bike
> With a special horn
> And you know it's Paul
> Who's passing you
> (Because of the horn)
> And because he calls
> (In a special way)
> "Come over" (and waves)
> Then blows the horn
> "Come over right now" (and smiles)
> "And play."

And you know what Paul
Is trying to say
When he waves and smiles and blows the horn
In that specially Paulish way?
It's "I'm your friend
And you're mine too
And there's something quite special
That's specially *you*."

Felice Holman

AGNES SNAGGLETOOTH

I don't like Agnes Snaggletooth.
How ever can I face her?
Why doesn't the Mafia rub her out
With a Snaggletooth-eraser?

I ape her grin behind her back.
I slide where she just slid.
I'd play with her, but she won't ask.
Well, I wouldn't if she did.

Why don't any *decent* kids move in?
This neighborhood's unlucky.
It's—who's that coming up our walk?
Not *her*! Oh, not that yukky—

Why, Agnes Sneedecker, you rang?
I didn't look for *you*.
Come out and play? Well I don't know.
Live here? I guess I do.

Who, me? *Me* help pull your loose tooth?
And try your racing bike?
Why Agnes Snag—why, who'd have thought—
Sure. Come in if you like.

X.J. Kennedy

THE MERRY PIEMAN'S SONG

"You are the cake of my endeavour, and my jelly-roll
  forever;
My tapioca-tartlet, my lemon-custard pie;
You're my candied fruit and spices, my juicy citron
  slices;
You're the darling, sugar-sprinkled apple-dumpling of
  my eye!"

John Bennett

THE FRESH AIR

The fresh air moves like water round a boat.
  The white clouds wander. Let us wander too.
The whining, wavering plover flap and float.
  That crow is flying after that cuckoo.
Look! Look! . . . They're gone. What are the great
  trees calling?
  Just come a little farther, by that edge
Of green, to where the stormy ploughland, falling
  Wave upon wave, is lapping to the hedge.
Oh, what a lovely bank! Give me your hand.
  Lie down and press your heart against the ground.
Let us both listen till we understand,
  Each through the other, every natural sound . . .
    I can't hear anything to-day, can you,
    But, far and near: "Cuckoo! Cuckoo!
    Cuckoo!"?

Harold Monro

A TIME TO TALK

When a friend calls to me from the road
And slows his horse to a meaning walk,
I don't stand still and look around
On all the hills I haven't hoed,
And shout from where I am, "What is it?"
No, not as there is a time to talk.
I thrust my hoe in the mellow ground,
Blade-end up and five feet tall,
And plod: I go up to the stone wall
For a friendly visit.

Robert Frost

WRITTEN AT THE PO-SHAN MONASTERY

I would rather be myself:
Why pretend being someone else?
Having traveled everywhere, I've returned to farming.
One pine, one bamboo, is a real friend;
Mountain birds, mountain flowers are my
brothers.

Hsin Ch'i-chi
translated by Irving Y. Lo

FRIENDSHIP

Like a quetzal plume, a fragrant flower,
friendship sparkles:
like heron plumes, it weaves itself into finery.
Our song is a bird calling out like a jingle:
how beautiful you make it sound!
Here, among flowers that enclose us,
among flowery boughs you are singing.

Aztec
translated by John Bierhorst

MILLIONS OF STRAWBERRIES

Marcia and I went over the curve,
Eating our way down
Jewels of strawberries we didn't deserve,
Eating our way down,
Till our hands were sticky, and our lips painted.
And over us the hot day fainted,
And we saw snakes,
And got scratched,
And a lust overcame us for the red unmatched
Small buds of berries,
Till we lay down—
Eating our way down—
And rolled in the berries like two little dogs,
Rolled
In the late gold.
And gnats hummed,
And it was cold,
And home we went, home without a berry,
Painted red and brown,
Eating our way down.

Genevieve Taggard

SIX
"We're Going to Be Good Friends"

THE FRIENDLY CINNAMON BUN

Shining in his stickiness and glistening with honey,
Safe among his sisters and his brothers on a tray,
With raisin eyes that looked at me as I put down my
    money,
There smiled a friendly cinnamon bun, and this I heard
    him say:

"It's a lovely, lovely morning, and the world's a lovely
    place;
I know it's going to be a lovely day.
I know we're going to be good friends; I like your honest
    face;
Together we might go a long, long way."

The baker's girl rang up the sale. "I'll wrap your bun,"
    said she.
"Oh no, you needn't bother," I replied.
I smiled back at that cinnamon bun and ate him, one
    two three,
And walked out with his friendliness inside.

Russell Hoban

SKILLY OOGAN

Skilly Oogan's no one you can see,
And no one else can be his friend but me.
Skilly lives where swallows live, away up high
Beneath the topmost eaves against the sky.
When all the world's asleep on moonlit nights,
Up on our roof he flies his cobweb kites.
He has an acorn boat that, when it rains,
He sails in gutters, even down the drains.
Sometimes he hides in letters that I write—
Snug in the envelope and out of sight,
On six-cent stamps he travels in all weathers
And with the midnight owl returns on silent feathers.
In summer time he rides the dragonflies
Above the pond, and looks in bullfrogs' eyes
For his reflection when he combs his hair.
And sometimes when I want him he's not there;
But mostly Skilly Oogan's where I think he'll be,
And no one even knows his name but me.

Russell Hoban

From I HAD A HIPPOPOTAMUS

I had a hippopotamus; I loved him as a friend;
But beautiful relationships are bound to have an end.
Time takes, alas! our joys from us and robs us of our
    blisses;
My hippopotamus turned out a hippopotamissis.

Patric Barrington

GIRAFFE

When I invite the Giraffe to dine,
I ask a carpenter friend of mine
To build a table so very tall
It takes up nearly the whole front hall.
The Giraffe and I do not need chairs:
He stands—I sit on the top of the stairs;
And we eat from crisp white paper plates
A meal of bananas, figs, and dates.

He whispers, when the table's clear,
Just loud enough for me to hear:
"Come one day soon to dine with me
And sit high up in a banyan tree
While Beasts of earth and sea and air
Gather all around us there,
All around the Unicorn
Who leads them with his lowered horn—

And we'll eat *without* white paper plates
A meal of bananas, figs, and dates."

William Jay Smith

From ON A BICYCLE

Under the dawn I wake my two-wheel friend.
Shouting in bed my mother says to me,
"Mind you don't clatter it going downstairs!"
I walk him down he springing step to step:
those tyres he has, if you pat him flat-handed
he'll bounce your hand. I mount with an air
and as light a pair of legs as you'll encounter,
slow into Sunday ride out of the gates,
roll along asphalt, press down on the pedals,
speeding,   fearless,

        ring,

              ring,

                    ring

> *Yevgeny Yevtushenko*
> *translated by Robin Milner-Gulland*
> *and Peter Levi, S.J.*

THE DUCK AND THE KANGAROO

I

Said the Duck to the Kangaroo,
  "Good gracious! how you hop
Over the fields, and the water too,
  As if you never would stop!
My life is a bore in this nasty pond;
And I long to go out in the world beyond:
  I wish I could hop like you,"
  Said the Duck to the Kangaroo.

II

"Please give me a ride on your back,"
  Said the Duck to the Kangaroo:
"I would sit quite still, and say nothing but 'Quack,'
  The whole of the long day through;
And we'd go the Dee, and the Jelly Bo Lee,
Over the land, and over the sea:
  Please take me a ride! oh, do!"
  Said the Duck to the Kangaroo.

III

Said the Kangaroo to the Duck,
  "This requires some little reflection.
Perhaps, on the whole, it might bring me luck:
  And there seems but one objection;
Which is, if you'll let me speak so bold,
Your feet are unpleasantly wet and cold,

And would probably give me the roo—
Matiz," said the Kangaroo.

IV

Said the Duck, "As I sate on the rocks,
   I have thought over that completely;
And I bought four pairs of worsted socks,
   Which fit my web-feet neatly;
And, to keep out the cold, I've bought a cloak;
And every day a cigar I'll smoke;
   And to follow my own dear true
   Love of a Kangaroo."

V

Said the Kangaroo, "I'm ready,
   All in the moonlight pale;
But to balance me well, dear Duck, sit steady,
   And quite at the end of my tail."
So away they went with a hop and a bound;
And they hopped the whole world three times round.
   And who so happy, oh! who,
   As the Duck and the Kangaroo?

Edward Lear

Moon
Have you met my mother?
Asleep in a chair there
Falling down hair.

Moon in the sky
Moon in the water
Have you met one another?
Moon face to moon face
Deep in that dark place
Suddenly bright.

Moon
Have you met my friend the night?

Karla Kuskin

In the fields of spring,
The nightingales sing.
To gain their friendship,
The plum blossoms have burst open
In the garden of my house.

Anonymous

From AUTUMN

Come! let us draw the curtains,
    heap up the fire and sit
hunched by the flame together,
    and make a friend of it . . .

Humbert Wolfe

SEVEN
"As Happy as Happy Could Be"

CELEBRATION

I shall dance tonight.
When the dusk comes crawling,
There will be dancing
    and feasting.
I shall dance with the others
    in circles,
      in leaps,
        in stomps.
Laughter and talk
    will weave into the night,
Among the fires
    of my people.
Games will be played
And I shall be
    a part of it.

Alonzo Lopez

CONJUGATION

I joy
You joy
He joys
We.
All of us
Will joy to be,
All of us
Will joy to sing
In the winter
In the spring,
All of us
Will joy to be.
I joy
You joy
He joys
We.

Patricia Hubbell

THE QUANGLE WANGLE'S HAT

I

On the top of the Crumpetty Tree
    The Quangle Wangle sat,
But his face you could not see,
    On account of his Beaver Hat.
For his Hat was a hundred and two feet wide,
With ribbons and bibbons on every side,
And bells, and buttons, and loops, and lace,
So that nobody ever could see the face
    Of the Quangle Wangle Quee.

II

The Quangle Wangle said
    To himself on the Crumpetty Tree,
    "Jam, and jelly, and bread
    Are the best of food for me!
But the longer I live on this Crumpetty Tree
The plainer than ever it seems to me
That very few people come this way
And that life on the whole is far from gay!"
    Said the Quangle Wangle Quee!"

III

But there came to the Crumpetty Tree
    Mr. and Mrs. Canary;
And they said, "Did ever you see
    Any spot so charmingly airy?

May we build a nest on your lovely Hat?
Mr. Quangle Wangle, grant us that!
O please let us come and build a nest
Of whatever material suits you best,
        Mr. Quangle Wangle Quee!"

IV

And besides, to the Crumpetty Tree
    Came the Stork, the Duck, and the Owl;
The Snail and the Bumble-Bee,
    The Frog and the Fimble Fowl
(The Fimble Fowl, with a Corkscrew leg);
And all of them said, "We humbly beg
We may build our homes on your lovely Hat,—
Mr. Quangle Wangle, grant us that!
        Mr. Quangle Wangle Quee!"

V

And the Golden Grouse came there,
    And the Pobble who has no toes,
And the small Olympian bear,
    And the Dong with a luminous nose.
And the Blue Baboon who played the flute,
And the Orient Calf from the Land of Tute,
And the Attery Squash, and the Bisky Bat,—
All came and built on the lovely Hat
        Of the Quangle Wangle Quee.

VI

And the Quangle Wangle said
    To himself on the Crumpetty Tree,
"When all these creatures move
    What a wonderful noise there'll be!"
And at night by the light of the Mulberry moon
They danced to the Flute of the Blue Baboon,
On the broad green leaves of the Crumpetty Tree,
And all were as happy as happy could be,
    With the Quangle Wangle Quee.

Edward Lear

There was a light pig from Montclair.
Dressed in feathers, she floated on air.
When the birds saw her frock,
They called, "Come, join our flock!"
Which she did, in the skies of Montclair.

Arnold Lobel

AT THE GARDEN GATE

Who so late
At the garden gate?
Emily, Kate,
And John.
"*John*,
Where have you been?
It's after six;
Supper is on,
And you've been gone
An hour, John!"
"We've been, we've been,
We've just been over
The field," said
John,
(Emily, Kate,
And John.)

Who so late
At the garden gate?
Emily, Kate,
And John.
"John,
What have you got?"
"A whopping toad.
Isn't he big?
He's a terrible
Load.

(We found him
A little ways
Up the road,"
Said Emily,
Kate,
And John.)

Who so late
At the garden gate?
Emily, Kate,
And John.
"*John,*
Put that thing down!
Do you want to get warts?"
(They all three have 'em
By last
Reports.)
Still, finding toads
Is the best of
Sports,
Say Emily,
Kate,
And John.

David McCord

THE ROSE ON MY CAKE

I went to a party,
A party for Pearly,
With presents and ice cream,
With favors and games.
I stayed very late
And I got there quite early.
I met all the guests
And I know all their names.
We sang and we jumped.
We jumped and we jostled.
We jostled and rustled
At musical chairs.
We ate up the cake
And we folded the candy in baskets
In napkins
We folded in squares.
We blew up balloons
And we danced without shoes.
We danced on the floor
And the rug and the bed.
We tripped and we trotted
In trios and twos.
And I neatly balanced myself
On my head.
Pearly just smiled
As she blew out the candles.
I gave the rose from my cake

To a friend,
Millicent Moss,
In her black patent sandals.
The trouble with parties is
All of them end.

Karla Kuskin

THE MARMALADE MAN
MAKES A DANCE TO MEND US

Tiger, Sunflowers, King of Cats,
Cow and Rabbit, mend your ways.
I the needle, you the thread—
follow me through mist and maze.

Fox and hound, go paw in paw.
Cat and rat, be best of friends.
Lamb and tiger, walk together.
Dancing starts where fighting ends.

Nancy Willard

The lands around my dwelling
Are more beautiful
From the day
When it is given me to see
Faces I have never seen before.
All is more beautiful,
All is more beautiful,
And life is Thankfulness.
These guests of mine
Make my house grand.

Eskimo
translated by
Knud Rasmussen

Put the pine tree in its pot by the doorway,
Set bamboo about the house,
Bring the crane and the tortoise to live in the house,
And long life and prosperity will dwell with you.

Eat beans, one more than the years of your age,
    and repeat,
"Out with the devils, in with good fortune."

Invite the ancestors to be your guests.
Set out food and drink for them.

Make calls on your friends and wish them peace and
    good health,

For this is the first moon,
The moon of three beginnings.
This is the holiday moon,
This is the friendly-moon.

Natalia Belting

TODAY IS SATURDAY

We started early, just as soon
As Doug had cleaned his room
And Ben had finished with his paper route.
We went the back way up to Walnut Street
And waited on the lawn 'till Mark came out.

And Mark had lots of money—birthday loot—
And he's the kind that likes to shoot the works,
And give his friends a treat.
So we went down to Gray's for Cheezy Chips
And pickles, and we sat outside along the curb to eat.
We finished up with ice cream—double dips,
With different flavors so we all could taste around,
And what we couldn't eat we gave to Jake,
That big old mutt who kind of lives down town.
We sat there on the curb and talked awhile,
About the kind of things that we might do.
But Mark had lost his softball, and for once
We didn't feel like fishing in the slough.

So we just wandered off along the path
That starts behind the school, without a plan.
We really still weren't going anywhere,
But when we felt like running, we just ran.

The day was like that—and the things we did
Just happened. And someway, that made them seem
More special than the things we mostly do,
A little bit like something from a dream,

I guess. It was an ordinary day.
Not cloudy, but the sun was kind of dusty gold,
And never very hot.

But everything we did was fun—and no one fought
For once. We laughed a lot
At things nobody else might even see.

No one would know what it was like I guess,
But guys like Doug and Ben and Mark and me.

Zilpha Keatley Snyder

THE SONG OF A DREAM

Now, my friends, please hear:
it is the song of a dream:
each spring the gold young corn
gives us life;
the ripened corn gives us refreshment;
to know that the hearts of our friends
are true is to put around us
a necklace of precious stones.

Aztec
translated by John Bierhorst

Sing hey! Sing hey!
For Christmas Day;
Twine mistletoe and holly,
For friendship glows
In winter snows,
And so let's all be jolly.

English, traditional

ALL ON A CHRISTMAS MORNING

I saw a robin
     and four of his friends,
All on a Christmas
     morning.
He came to the road
     where the woodland
          ends,
And with him were four of his high-
     stepping friends,
All on a Christmas
     morning.

His head was cocked
     and his breast was
          red,
All on a Christmas morning.
I hope he has a warm
     place for a bed
And can ask his friends home
     to a barn or a shed,
All on a Christmas morning.

I hope he has
     berries and seeds
          to eat,
All on a Christmas
     morning.
Good luck to you,

robin! And
many a treat
For you and your friends!
Oh! plenty to eat!
*On a cold, bright Christmas
morning!*

Elizabeth Coatsworth

EIGHT
"The Scratches Are Always There"

Friendship is like china	*Autograph verse*
Misery is when your	*Langston Hughes*
As the sun came up, a ball of red	*Chinese Mother Goose*
Elizabeth Cried	*Eleanor Farjeon*
There was a young lady of Kent	*Anonymous*
Friendship	*Shel Silverstein*
Fifty-fifty	*Carl Sandburg*
i have friends	*Cheryl Thornton*
You Smiled	*Calvin O'John*
Sensitive Sydney	*Wallace Irwin*

Friendship is like china
Costly and rare.
Tho' it can be mended
The scratches are always there.

Autograph Verse

Misery is when your
very best friend
calls you a name she really
didn't mean to call you at all.

Misery is when you call
your very best friend a name
you didn't mean to call her, either

Langston Hughes

As the sun came up, a ball of red,
I followed my friend wherever he led.
He thought his fast horse would leave me behind,
But I rode a dragon as swift as the wind!

Chinese Mother Goose
translated by Robert Wyndham

ELIZABETH CRIED

Elizabeth cried
Because I came.
I never tried
To play a game,
I ate my meat
And I looked away—
Till Elizabeth's feet
Ran up, to stay.

We played a game
All over the place,
She said my name,
And I washed her face,
I gave her a ride—
Till my time was spent,
And Elizabeth cried
Because I went.

Eleanor Farjeon

There was a young lady of Kent,
Who always said just what she meant.
People said, "She's a dear—
So unique—so sincere."
But they shunned her by common consent.

Anonymous

FRIENDSHIP

I've discovered a way to stay friends forever—
There's really nothing to it.
I simply tell you what to do
And you do it!

Shel Silverstein

FIFTY-FIFTY

What is there for us two
to split fifty-fifty,
to go halvers on?
>A Bible, a deck of cards?
>a farm, a frying pan?
>a porch, front steps to sit on?

How can we be pals
>when you speak English
>and I speak English
>and you never understand me
>and I never understand you?

Carl Sandburg

i have friends
like staircases—
they wind and wind
with many, tiny narrow
steps
up and up
except they
always
stop at
just one room
at "their" top
and close
their door
tightly to all
others.

Cheryl Thornton

YOU SMILED

You smiled,
I smiled,
So we're both happy,
But deep down inside
There is hatred between us.
Let's not show our inside feeling
    to one another;
    Just keep on smiling
    Until we smile away our hate.

Calvin O'John

SENSITIVE SYDNEY

'Twas all along the Binder Line
    A-sailin' of the sea
That I fell out with Sydney Bryne
    And Sid fell out with me.

He spoke o' me as "pie-faced squid"
    In a laughin' sort o' way,
And I, in turn, had spoke o' Sid
    As a "bow-legg'd bunch o' hay."

He'd mentioned my dishonest phiz
    And called me "blattin' calf"—
We both enjoyed this joke o' his
    And had a hearty laugh.

But when I up and says to him,
    "Yer necktie ain't on straight,"
"I didn't think ye'd say that, Jim,"
    He hissed with looks o' hate.

And then he lit a fresh segar
    And turned away and swore—
So I knowed I'd brung the joke too far
    And we wasn't friends no more.

Wallace Irwin

NINE
"Missing You"

I CANNOT FORGET YOU

No matter how hard I try to forget you, you always
    come back to my thoughts.
When you hear me singing I am really crying for you.

Makah
translated by Frances Densmore

MISSING YOU

Once we laughed together
By the river side
And watched the little waves
Watched the waves.

Now I walk
Along the bank.
The water's very blue
And I am walking by the waves
Walking by the waves
                    Missing you.

Charlotte Zolotow

THE TAMARINDO PUPPY

The Tamarindo puppy
is a very nice puppy
Is a muy lindo puppy
Whom we visit every day.

But the Tamarindo puppy,
When we went there Monday morning,
The Tamarindo puppy
Aw
Had gone away.

What happened to the puppy,
The Tamarindo puppy,
Lindo, lindo puppy,
Whom we saw every day?

Did somebody see him
And say, "Oh, how darling!"
Did somebody see him
And say, "¡Ay, qué lindo!"
Did somebody see him
And take him home to play?

Does he like his new home,
The Tamarindo puppy?
Does he like his new friends,
Muy lejos, far away?

Or does he miss the breeze
In the Tamarindo trees

And his friends who came to visit him
Every single day?

Charlotte Pomerantz

POEM

I loved my friend.
He went away from me.
There's nothing more to say.
The poem ends,
Soft as it began—
I loved my friend.

Langston Hughes

THANK YOU FOR YOUR LETTER

The letter you sent me touched my heart
The paper was decorated with a pair of magpies.
Now I think always of the magpies who fly with joined
    wings.
I do not mind that your letter was so short.

Ch'ao Li-houa
translated by Kenneth Rexroth

LETTER TO A FRIEND

Come soon.

Everything is lusting
for light,
thrusting
up
up
splitting the earth,
opening flaring fading,
seed
into shoot
bud
into flower,
nothing
beyond its hour.

Come soon.

The apple bloom has melted
like
spring snow.

The lilac
changed the air
surprising
every breath.

Now
low in the field

wild strawberries
fatten.

Come soon.

It's a matter of
life.
And Death.

Lilian Moore

LETTER FROM SICILY

We haven't eaten the grape
from the vineyard by the sea.
That creek where we used to wash
the grape is now dry;
the water loses itself
in the fields.
Return, dear friend,
for one more picnic
on a hill,
under the stars,
where we may dance.

Emanuel di Pasquale

TOO SLOW

Too slow
all mail from you.
Freight mail's
I can't wait mail.
The fastest rail mail,
snail mail.
The swiftest jet mail,
still not yet mail.
How about a telegram?
Or better still, come home.

Lillian Morrison

LITTLE ELEGY

Withouten you
No rose can grow;
No leaf be green
If never seen
Your sweetest face;
No bird have grace
Or power to sing;
Or anything
Be kind, or fair,
And you nowhere.

Elinor Wylie

SEPARATION

Your absence has gone through me
Like thread through a needle.
Everything I do is stitched with its color.

W. S. Merwin

Remember the M,
Remember the E,
Put them together,
Remember ME.

Autograph Verse

A PARTING

Friend, I have watched you down the mountain
Till now in the dark I close my thatch door. . . .
Grasses return again green in the spring,
But O my Prince of Friends, do you?

Wang Wei
translated by Witter Bynner
and Kiang Kan-Hu

❧ INDEX OF TITLES ❧

❧ INDEX OF FIRST LINES ❧

. . .

❧ INDEX OF AUTHORS ❧

❧ INDEX OF TRANSLATORS ❧

DATE DUE			

808.81 Livingston, Myra
LIV   Cohn
           I like you, if you
           like me

Bound to Stay Bound Books, Inc.